Disney PRINCESS

Beauty
and the Beast

PaRragon

Bath • New York • Cologne • Melbourne • Delhi
Hong Kong • Shenzhen • Singapore

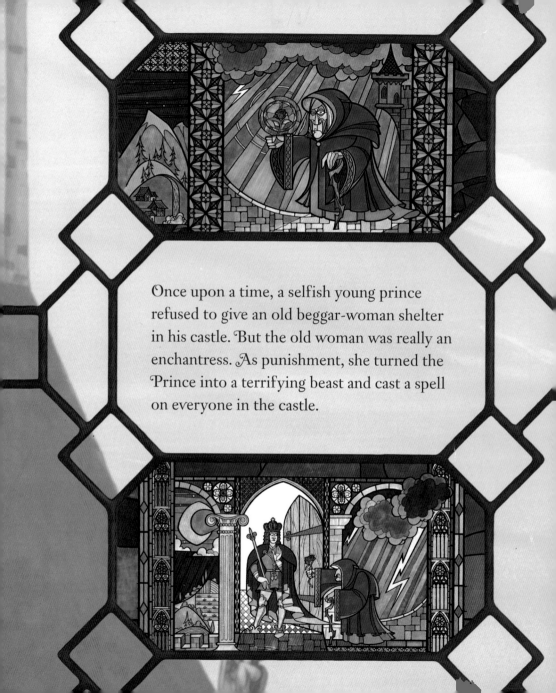

Once upon a time, a selfish young prince refused to give an old beggar-woman shelter in his castle. But the old woman was really an enchantress. As punishment, she turned the Prince into a terrifying beast and cast a spell on everyone in the castle.

Giving the Beast a magic rose she said,
"This will bloom until your twenty-first year.
If you learn to love another and earn that
person's love before the last petal falls, the
spell will be broken. If not, you will remain
a Beast forever."

In a sleepy village nearby, an eccentric inventor named Maurice lived with his beautiful daughter Belle.

Gaston, a strong and handsome young man from the village, had decided that he wanted to make Belle his wife.

"After all," he told his friend Lefou, "she's the best-looking girl in town."

Gaston arrived at Belle's house, confident that she would agree to marry him. But, when he asked her, Belle refused him without a second thought. She knew she could never marry someone as rude and bad-mannered as Gaston!

One day Maurice
set off for a fair with his
latest invention. As night fell he lost his
way and had to seek refuge in the Beast's castle.
Maurice was welcomed by some friendly,
enchanted servants, a candelabra named Lumiere
and a clock named Cogsworth.

But the Beast was angry when he discovered
a stranger in his home and he threw Maurice into
the dungeon.

When Maurice's horse returned home alone,
Belle set off at once to search for her father.
    Belle found her father trapped
in the freezing dungeon.
    "Oh, Papa," she cried, "we
must get you out of here!"

Sensing danger, Belle turned round.
There was the Beast, towering over her and
growling loudly.

"Please let my father go," Belle pleaded.

Finally, when Belle offered to take her father's
place, the Beast agreed – with one condition.

"You must promise to stay here forever,"
the Beast said.

The Beast showed Belle to her room.

"You can go anywhere in the castle,"
he told her, "except the West Wing.
That is forbidden!"

Poor Belle was miserable! She missed
her father and her home. The castle's
enchanted objects prepared a wonderful
meal for her and tried to cheer her up with
their singing and dancing.

Later that night Belle wandered through the castle to the
West Wing. There, among broken furniture and cracked
mirrors, she found the magic rose, its petals drooping sadly.
    Just as Belle reached out to touch the rose,
the Beast burst in howling with rage.
Terrified, Belle ran out into the snowy night.

Belle leaped on to her father's
horse and set off into the dark forest.
Suddenly, she was surrounded
by a pack of vicious, hungry wolves.
Just as the wolves closed in for the
kill, the Beast appeared and drove
the wolves away.

The wolves had injured the
Beast in the battle. Belle took the
Beast back to the castle and gently
tended his bleeding wounds.
The Beast seemed quite different now
and she was no longer frightened of him.

Meanwhile, at the village tavern, Gaston was still brooding over Belle, even though his friends did their best to cheer him up.

Suddenly, the door burst open and Maurice raced in. "Help!" he cried. "Belle is being held prisoner by a monstrous Beast!"

The men in the tavern burst out laughing. They thought Maurice was mad! But Gaston smiled to himself. He had thought of a wicked plan to make Belle marry him.

As the days passed, Belle and the Beast spent more and more time together. The enchanted servants were delighted. They were certain that Belle would fall in love with their master and break the spell. But time was running out. Each day more petals fell from the magic rose.

One evening, after dining and dancing together, the Beast and Belle sat out on the terrace in the cool night air.

"Are you happy here, Belle?" asked the Beast.

"Yes," replied Belle. "I just wish I could see my father again."

"You can," said the Beast, and he gave Belle a magic mirror. "This will show you whatever you wish."

"Oh, thank you!" exclaimed Belle. But, as she gazed into it, Belle saw her father lost and trembling with cold as he searched for her!

Although the Beast loved Belle,
he knew he had to let her go to her father.

"Take the mirror with you," the Beast
said sadly, "so you can remember me."

Belle set off from the castle and soon found
Maurice and brought him safely home.

The next day Gaston arrived at Belle's house with
a crowd of villagers. He said that Maurice would be
taken to an asylum unless Belle agreed to marry him.

"My father's not mad!" cried Belle.
"He must be," said Lefou.
"He was raving about a
monstrous beast!"
Belle held up the magic
mirror to help prove that her
father wasn't mad. The crowd
shouted with fear when they
saw the image of Beast.

Gaston led the men up to the castle to attack the Beast. Cogsworth and the enchanted servants fought bravely against the villagers. But the Beast missed Belle and was too heartbroken to fight. Gaston overpowered the Beast and drove him on to the castle roof.

Only when he heard Belle's voice did the Beast look up.
"You came back!" he cried, rushing to embrace Belle.
Seeing his chance, Gaston drew his dagger and stabbed the Beast.
But as the Beast collapsed, Gaston tripped – and fell tumbling from
the roof.

Belle ran to the wounded Beast and bent to kiss him. "You can't die," sobbed Belle. "I love you!"

As Belle spoke, the last rose petal fell. Suddenly, magical sparkles began to swirl around the Beast. He rose into the air and in a shower of light the Beast began to transform.

Magic swirled above the castle as the servants were transformed, too. The spell was broken!

At last the Prince had found his true love. As the sun burst through the clouds, they knew they would live together in happiness for ever after.